Off Off Broadway Festival Plays

Thirty-Seventh Series

ANNIVERSARY
by Rachel Bonds

NAKED EYES
by Dean Imperial

FORGETTING TO REMEMBER
by Greg Kalleres

WOLF PLAY
by Claire Kiechel

MISSED CONNECTION
by Catya McMullen

EDISON/TESLA: BRIAN/DAVE
by Darren Miller & Kevin Mead

A SAMUEL FRENCH ACTING EDITION

SAMUEL
FRENCH

FOUNDED 1830

SAMUELFRENCH.COM
SAMUELFRENCH-LONDON.CO.UK

ISBN 978-0-573-70204-4

www.SamuelFrench.com
www.SamuelFrench-London.co.uk

FOR PRODUCTION ENQUIRIES

UNITED STATES AND CANADA
Info@SamuelFrench.com
1-866-598-8449

UNITED KINGDOM AND EUROPE
Theatre@SamuelFrench-London.co.uk
020-7255-4302

Each title is subject to availability from Samuel French, depending upon country of performance. Please be aware that *ANNIVERSARY, NAKED EYES, FORGETTING TO REMEMBER, WOLF PLAY, MISSED CONNECTION,* and *EDISON/TESLA: BRIAN/DAVE* may not be licensed by Samuel French in your territory. Professional and amateur producers should contact the nearest Samuel French office or licensing partner to verify availability.

MUSIC USE NOTE

IMPORTANT BILLING AND CREDIT REQUIREMENTS

OOBB

SAMUEL FRENCH
OFF OFF BROADWAY
SHORT PLAY FESTIVAL

The Beckett Theatre
Theatre Row

October 23-28, 2012

SINCE 1975

FOREWORD

We are honored to have these six daring and inspirational playwrights as the winners of our 2012 Off Off Broadway Short Play Festival. This year we had over 900 submissions from around the world. We thank all of these gifted playwrights for sharing their talent with us and welcome each one into this elite group of emerging playwrights.

The vital relationship between playwright and theatre is one that we know well at Samuel French. Whether producing a Tony-winning play or developing a new work, theatre companies play a vital role in cultivating new audiences and communicating a playwright's vision. We commend them for this mission and thank each of the forty producing companies involved in the 2012 Festival for their tireless contribution and dedication to their playwright.

Perhaps the most challenging part of the OOB Festival is our production week. From our initial pool of Final Forty playwrights, we ultimately select six plays for publication and representation by Samuel French. Of course, we can't make our selection alone, and so we enlist some brilliant minds within the theatre industry to help us in this process. Each night of the Festival, we have an esteemed group of judges consisting of a Samuel French playwright, a theatrical agent, and an artistic director. We thank them for their support, insight, and commitment to the art of playwriting.

Samuel French is a 182-year-old company rich in history while at the same time dedicated to the future. We are constantly striving to develop ground-breaking methods which will better connect playwright and producer. With a team committed to developing new products and services, outreach to theatres, and our new interactive website, we are boldly embracing our role in this industry as bridge between playwright and theatre.

On behalf of our board of directors, the entire Samuel French team in our New York, Los Angeles, and London offices, the over 10,000 playwrights, composers and lyricists that we publish and represent...we present you with the seven winners of the 2012 Samuel French Off Off Broadway Short Play Festival. Get ready to be inspired.

The Festival Organizers
Samuel French 37th Annual Off Off Broadway Short Play Festival
Samuel French, Inc.

The Samuel French Off Off Broadway Short Play Festival started in 1975 and is one of the nation's most established and highly regarded short play festivals. During the course of the Festival's 37 years, over 500 theatre companies and schools participated in the Festival, including companies from coast to coast as well as abroad from Canada, Singapore, and the United Kingdom. Over the years, more than 200 submitted plays have been published, with many of the participants becoming established, award-winning playwrights.

CONTENTS

ANNIVERSARY

Rachel Bonds

For Dad and for Linsay

Anniversary received its premiere production at The Ensemble Studio Theatre in its Marathon of One Act Plays 2010. It was directed by Linsay Firman. The cast was as follows:

PENELOPE . . . . Julei Fitzpatrick

MATT . . . . Jerry Richardson

CAROLINE . . . . Claire Siebers

NEAL . . . . Eddie Boroevich

CHARACTERS

PENELOPE – 29-to-early 30's
MATT – early-to-mid 30's
CAROLINE – 29-to-early 30's
NEAL – 29-to-early 30's

PLAYWRIGHT'S NOTE

Caroline and Neal should be overwhelming, a bit theatrical; their enthusiasm should fill the room and surround Penelope.

I imagine this as a very stark world, with little furniture and props. Every setting should be created as simply as possible.

ABOUT THE PLAYWRIGHT

Rachel Bonds' plays have been developed at New Georges, Ars Nova, Ensemble Studio Theatre, LaMaMa, The Flea, Playwrights Horizons, Williamstown Theater Festival, The Greenpoint Division, The Sewanee Writers' Conference, The Atlantic Center for the Arts, LA's Echo Theater, and Gotham Stage Company. She is currently an affiliated artist with New Georges, a member of EST's Youngblood, a member of Ars Nova's Play Group, and a Playwriting Mentor in PEN American Center's Prison Writing Program. Rachel is a graduate of Brown University.

(**PENELOPE** *in a pool of light. Stark and bright.*)

PENELOPE. On the anniversary of your death I decide to go to the mediocre deli on the corner for lunch. I don't want to taste any real food tastes. I don't want to enjoy the rich flavors of roasted beet salad or pan seared tuna steak because I just want to eat grey roast beef on a plain white bun and have the whole event be a big grey blur on this long grey day.

(The light shifts to the strange flourescent light of a mediocre deli; there is the faint murmuring of Top 40 hits.)

MATT. Do you mind if I sit here?

PENELOPE. What?

MATT. There's no other free seats.

PENELOPE. Oh – sure.

*(They sit in silence for a moment. **PENELOPE** stares at her sandwich.)*

MATT. This doesn't seem like your kind of place.

PENELOPE. Why?

MATT. I don't know. You don't look like you eat a lot of crappy deli meat.

PENELOPE. Oh. Well.

MATT. I'm Matt.

PENELOPE. Hi Matt.

MATT. Hi.

You're not going to tell me your name?

PENELOPE. Umm.

MATT. I told you mine.

PENELOPE. Yes. You did.

MATT. You can give me a fake one.

PENELOPE. A fake name?

MATT. Yeah.

(She peers at him.)

PENELOPE. Okay. Debra.

MATT. Hey Deb.

(He holds out his hand.)

PENELOPE. Debra.

MATT. Debra. It's nice to meet you.

(She hesitates, then shakes his hand.)

PENELOPE. You too.

MATT. You've got a very firm handshake, Debra.

PENELOPE. Thanks. So do you.

MATT. I think I've seen you before.

PENELOPE. Yeah?

MATT. You live nearby. Right? I think I've seen you.

PENELOPE. I don't know.

MATT. You don't live nearby?

PENELOPE. I'm sorry. I just want to sit here and eat this grey roast beef and not have to talk to anyone.

MATT. Oh. Okay. I'm sorry.

PENELOPE. *(gathering herself up to leave)* No, it's okay – I just really really want to be left alone today.

MATT. Sure – you don't have to leave. /I'll move or –

PENELOPE. No, it's fine I need to go anyway, so.

MATT. Okay. Sorry.

It was nice to meet you.

PENELOPE. *(leaving)* Yeah.

***

(the sounds of a big party in a small apartment)

PENELOPE. Two months after the anniversary of your death I run into Matt at a party. I really didn't want to go to this party. But Caroline and Neal insisted. They've just gotten engaged.

CAROLINE. Penelope! You made it!

NEAL. Thank you for coming –

CAROLINE. It's so good to see you –

NEAL. You look fantastic –

CAROLINE & NEAL. You look really fantastic.

PENELOPE. Congratulations.

CAROLINE & NEAL. Thank you!

CAROLINE. Yeah – we're finally taking the plunge. Oh! – And we /decided

NEAL. We decided we're doing the wedding in Mexico!

CAROLINE. On the beach!

NEAL. While the sun is setting!

CAROLINE. And then we'll all go swimming!

PENELOPE. Wow.

NEAL. It's going to be awesome –

CAROLINE. It's going to be gorgeous –

CAROLINE & NEAL. You have to come!

PENELOPE. It sounds really fun.

CAROLINE. You really look great, Penny.

NEAL. Put down your coat –

CAROLINE. Go have a drink –

NEAL. Go have some food –

CAROLINE & NEAL. *Please* have some food – we got way too much food!

PENELOPE. Okay.

CAROLINE & NEAL. Have a good time!

PENELOPE. Thank you.

Two months after the anniversary of your death I proceed to drink way too much at our friends' from college engagement party.

MATT. Hello.

PENELOPE. Oh. Hi.

MATT. Do you remember me?

PENELOPE. From the day of the grey roast beef.

MATT. Matt.

PENELOPE. Matt. Right.

MATT. How are you?

PENELOPE. Ohhhh. I've had four gin and tonics.

MATT. Okay. So, pretty good?

PENELOPE. Pretty good, yeah. On the outside.

MATT. And on the inside?

PENELOPE. Oh – I'm like a huuuuuuge pile of ashes. And dust. And rubble.

MATT. You're in ruins?

PENELOPE. Yes.

MATT. I'm sorry to hear that.

PENELOPE. Ehh. I'm used to it.

MATT. I'm sorry to hear that as well.

PENELOPE. You have a very kind, very good heart.

MATT. Thank you.

PENELOPE. It's in very good condition.

MATT. Um – thank you.

PENELOPE. I mean it's in good working order. Not in ruins.

MATT. I see.

PENELOPE. I bet if we opened you up and took out your heart and looked at it, it would be bright red and royal blue and full of blood and blindly and happily pumping along.

MATT. Maybe.

PENELOPE. It doesn't yet know what could become of it.

MATT. Yikes.

PENELOPE. You're friends with Caroline and Neal?

MATT. I work with Caroline, actually.

PENELOPE. Oh. Saving the children?

MATT. Um – kind of. It's a human rights organization, so…

PENELOPE. Oh. Saving everyone.

(He shrugs.)

They're getting married.

MATT. I know.

PENELOPE. I knew them both before they even knew each other.

MATT. Oh yeah?

PENELOPE. Yes. It's funny to think about.

MATT. Yes.

PENELOPE. Time passes and passes and passes.

MATT. Yes…

I asked Caroline about you.

PENELOPE. You did?

MATT. She told me your name.

PENELOPE. Oh.

MATT. Your real name.

PENELOPE. Oh.

MATT. Penelope?

PENELOPE. Yes.

MATT. That's a beautiful name.

PENELOPE. Thank you.

MATT. Why are you in ruins, Penelope?

PENELOPE. Oh shit.

MATT. What?

PENELOPE. I shouldn't have – . Said that.

MATT. It's all right.

PENELOPE. I don't need saving.

MATT. What?

PENELOPE. I don't need saving.

MATT. All right.

PENELOPE. You seem like you have the rescue complex.

MATT. I don't think so.

Mm.

Maybe.

PENELOPE. Yeah. Maybe.

(She grows quiet.)

Don't rescue me, okay?

MATT. Okay.

PENELOPE. Okay.

MATT. Have you really had four gin and tonics?

PENELOPE. This is five.

MATT. I want to ask you something, but I don't know if I should.

PENELOPE. Because I'm drunk?

MATT. Noo/oo…

PENELOPE. You can ask me.

MATT. Mmm… *(He squints at her, hesitating. Then, formally:)* Will you go out to dinner with me, Penelope?

PENELOPE. I don't know.

MATT. Okay.

Why?

PENELOPE. I have to think about it.

MATT. Well. Okay…How about /this –

PENELOPE. You're making plans.

MATT. How about – I'll get your number from Caroline. Then I'll call you in…how long?

PENELOPE. Eight days.

MATT. Eight days. Okay. I'll get your number from Caroline and I'll call you in eight days and ask you if you would like to go to dinner with me.

PENELOPE. Okay.

MATT. Good.

Here. Let's shake on it.

(He holds out his hand.)

(She takes it.)

PENELOPE. *(still shaking his hand)* I have the spins, Matt.

MATT. Uh oh.

Here.

(He guides her to a chair.)

PENELOPE. Thanks.

MATT. Wait. One sec.

(He disappears.)

(He reappears holding a piece of bread.)

Here.

PENELOPE. You brought me bread.

MATT. I think you should eat something.

PENELOPE. I'm sorry I was rude to you that day.

MATT. That's all right.

PENELOPE. *(taking the bread)* Thank you Matt with the good heart.

MATT. You're welcome.

(She eats the bread very slowly. He stands beside her. They stare out at the rest of the party swirling around them, lights spinning across their faces.)

***

(Early, early morning. **PENELOPE** *sits in an armchair.*
MATT *sleeps on the floor.)*

PENELOPE. Four months and two weeks after the
anniversary of your death I sleep with Matt. On the
living room floor. Between the couch and the coffee
table.

I don't tell him it's because using the furniture feels
like some kind of betrayal.

MATT. Hey.

PENELOPE. Hey.

MATT. You okay?

PENELOPE. Yeah. I'm okay.

Are you okay?

MATT. Very.

PENELOPE. Okay.

MATT. What time is it?

PENELOPE. Ummm…I don't know. Early.

MATT. I don't remember falling asleep.

PENELOPE. Yeah.

MATT. Let's go out and eat enormous amounts of breakfast.

PENELOPE. Okay.

MATT. Don't you love getting up when it's really really
early?

PENELOPE. Sometimes.

MATT. I love that feeling. It's like, maybe only a couple
other people in the city are up right now and the light
is strange and it feels like a great secret. Right?

PENELOPE. Yeah. Yeah.

It reminds me of long car trips.

MATT. Yeahhh…

When I was in high school, there were these horses
that my dad would take care of…but their owners lived
way, way out, like two and a half hours away, and he
would get up really really early on Saturday morning
and drive out there to take care of these horses. And at

some point…I don't remember why…I started going with him – so we'd get up around four and get in his truck around 4:30 and drive out to these people's farm. And it was always dark and cold out and there was hardly anyone else on the road, maybe one or two other cars, and we would drive way far out there into the country, drinking coffee out of thermos tops and we were really really quiet and we didn't say anything, and the sky was that deep navy blue that it gets in the winter and I was always wearing a huge sweatshirt with the hood pulled up, and I would stare out the window at all the blurry fields speeding by and we would just drive and drive through the morning like that.

But I can still feel that feeling, you know? Like I can actually *feel* what it *felt like* to be sitting there at 4:30 in the morning in the truck in the dark with my dad.

Isn't it weird that some memories are like that – like, it's not really an image I'm remembering, it's an entire feeling. Do you know? It's like it takes over my entire body, this memory…

(**PENELOPE** *is crying, very quietly.* **MATT** *sits up.*)

MATT. Are you crying?

PENELOPE. *(wiping her face)* Agh – sorry.

MATT. *(getting up)* Are you okay?

PENELOPE. Yes yes sorry sorry.

MATT. What happened?

PENELOPE. *(laughing/crying)* I don't know.
Shit.
Were they sick?

MATT. Who? The horses?

PENELOPE. *(laughing/crying)* Yeah.

MATT. Oh! No. My dad just used to give them their regular check-ups.

PENELOPE. Oh.

MATT. One of them had a hurt leg once, I guess.

PENELOPE. Yeah.

MATT. But he was okay.

PENELOPE. Yeah.

MATT. You were worried about the horses?

PENELOPE. I don't know.

MATT. I'm – /sorry –

PENELOPE. No, no – it's okay.

Shit.

Sorry.

You made me homesick.

(She laughs.)

MATT. I think you're very beautiful, Penelope.

PENELOPE. Ohh…

MATT. I do.

(She wipes her face.)

Did. Did this freak you out?

(He gestures to the floor between the couch and the coffee table.)

PENELOPE. Ummm…

MATT. Do you want me to – do something differently? Or –

PENELOPE. No – no! You're great.

MATT. Okay.

But.

You were just crying.

PENELOPE. I /know.

MATT. Which doesn't exactly inspire confidence.

PENELOPE. It's not – Ughhhhhhh /shit.

MATT. Unless you're emotionally overcome by my sexual prowess.

PENELOPE. I get sad sometimes.

MATT. Okay.

PENELOPE. So…I don't know. I guess, don't take it personally?

MATT. Okay…

That might be difficult.

(She shrugs, her palms out.)

Do you want to just go get breakfast?

PENELOPE. Yeah.

MATT. Okay. Let's go get breakfast.

(He holds out his hand.)

(She takes it.)

(They both stand. And stare at each other.)

***

(A beach. The end of evening.)

PENELOPE. One month and three days before the anniversary of your death Matt with the good heart takes me away to Montauk for the weekend.

MATT. Let's just sleep out here tonight.

PENELOPE. Perfect.

MATT. We'll just curl up on our blanket and sleep right here.

PENELOPE. The bed and breakfast guy will not like that one bit.

He looks like a fisherman from a horror movie.

MATT. Yes! He is very...weathered.

PENELOPE. I think he has a glass eye.

MATT. What! No.

PENELOPE. He does! I think he does.

MATT. How do you know?

PENELOPE. His left eye is very weird and...blank-looking. Like there's nothing behind it.

MATT. Oh God.

PENELOPE. And if he finds out we took his blanket out to this beach, he's going to hunt us down in the middle of the night.

MATT. With a rusty hook.

PENELOPE. Yes.

MATT. And hack into our flesh.

PENELOPE. Yes.

MATT. And use us as bait.

PENELOPE. Yes!

(They laugh. They kiss.)

MATT. Are you having a good time?

PENELOPE. Of course.

MATT. I want you to have a good time.

PENELOPE. I am.

MATT. Okay.

PENELOPE. What?

MATT. I want you to be happy.

PENELOPE. I know you do.

MATT. Are you?

PENELOPE. Matt.

MATT. What?

PENELOPE. I'm…content.

MATT. Okay.

PENELOPE. But…I think we have different versions of "happy." I think I feel happy in moments, and then those moments pass. And then there are new moments.

MATT. Well, I'm happy.

PENELOPE. Well – good.

MATT. I feel pretty much in a constant state of euphoria.

PENELOPE. Really?

MATT. With you, yes.

PENELOPE. Oh.

MATT. Except you get that look.

PENELOPE. What look.

MATT. You go very far away.

PENELOPE. Oh.

MATT . And I don't think you want me to know where you go.

PENELOPE. It's not that I don't *want* you to –

MATT. It's okay. I just want you to know that I want to know. Where you go. And that I would go with you if you wanted.

PENELOPE. Matt with the good heart.

MATT. Don't do that.

PENELOPE. What?

MATT. Treat me like I'm naïve.

PENELOPE. That's not /what I meant.

MATT. Like I've lived some untouched life or something.

PENELOPE. Well. I mean. You have.

MATT. What?

PENELOPE. I mean – Your parents are still married. You're good-looking and everyone likes you. You're smart and your siblings are all really nice and your family is really nice and everyone's healthy and good-natured and every single one of your grandparents is still alive and everything is always very nice.

MATT. That's not fair, Penelope.

PENELOPE. Well.

MATT. Everyone has their shit.

PENELOPE. What shit have you dealt with?

MATT. Seriously?

PENELOPE. Name something hard you've had to go through.

MATT. What the fuck?

PENELOPE. Name one thing.

MATT. You're being kind of a dick, Penelope.

PENELOPE. A dick?!

MATT. What do you want me to say? My sister was bulimic for a while. My mom gets depressed sometimes. My brother smokes too much pot. Is that good?

PENELOPE. I'm just saying –

MATT. This is really petty.

PENELOPE. I'm saying I've dealt – I'm still dealing with something very difficult and I sometimes think you cannot possibly understand it.

MATT. I'm trying to understand it. I've tried really hard / to be patient.

PENELOPE. Yes, I know…

MATT. But yes – it's getting to be really difficult when you spend three days in bed not talking to me or when you're happy one minute and then sobbing on the floor the next.

PENELOPE. Well, *yeah* – I'M SAD!

MATT. I KNOW! I know I know I know. You've made that abundantly clear.

Just. Don't accuse me – don't blame me for not having had some horrible tragedy in my life.

PENELOPE. *(quiet)* Okay.

I'm sorry I'm so fucked up.

MATT. You're not fucked up. Don't be so dramatic.

(They stare at the ocean.)

PENELOPE. I want to go home.

(He nods.)

(The light changes.)

***

(The strange light of a mediocre deli; a faint murmuring of Top 40 hits. **PENELOPE** *sits alone, staring at a sandwich.)*

PENELOPE. On the anniversary of your death I go back to the mediocre deli on the corner for lunch.

I think maybe Matt will walk in the door.

He doesn't.

(The light changes as **PENELOPE** *sits alone, the hours passing and passing.)*

***

(The sounds of rush hour. **PENELOPE** *stands nervously on the city street.)*

PENELOPE. Two months and 4 days after the anniversary of your death I wait for Matt on the street outside of his office.

*(***MATT*** *appears on the street, leaving work.)*

Hi.

MATT. *(surprised)* Hey.

PENELOPE. I called you – but.

MATT. I know.

PENELOPE. So I thought. I could come here.

MATT. Okay.

PENELOPE. And see you.

MATT. Well. You see me.

PENELOPE. I miss you. Very much.

MATT. Okay.

PENELOPE. Please talk to me.

MATT. You came to see me. You talk to me.

PENELOPE. Okay.

Um.

I'm going to try to explain this.

MATT. Okay.

PENELOPE. Okay, so. Okay – it's like – . Inside me is an enormous map. And there's one place where I have… where I put this thing that happened to me. And it's… it's Iowa. Okay? So there are some days when I can be standing in New York and looking out and I'll see Iowa out of the corner of my eye, and I'll know it's out there, but I'm okay. I'm standing in New York. But then there are some days when Iowa starts overflowing; it grows and grows and grows and washes over the entire map and then I'm swimming through Iowa and I can't be anywhere but Iowa.

But you're standing in New York…

PENELOPE. *(cont.)* And now…when I'm swimming in Iowa, I want to be standing with you. I'm trying to get back to you.

And I think. It will get easier. And. Eventually, I'll just be able to stand in New York and simply see Iowa out there in the corner of my eye.

So.

MATT. So.

PENELOPE. So. I guess I'm asking you to – wait. For me.

(They stare at each other.)

MATT. You can't shut down and not talk to me for days because you're in Iowa.

PENELOPE. Okay.

MATT. You have to tell me…what it's like there.

PENELOPE. Lots of cows.

MATT. I'm serious.

PENELOPE. I know.

MATT. You have to talk to me.

PENELOPE. Okay.

MATT. Okay.

(They look at each other. The sounds of rush hour.)

***

*(**PENELOPE** in a pool of light. Perhaps the last of evening or the first of the morning, dim and warm.)*

PENELOPE. On the anniversary of your death Matt and I move to a third floor walk-up in Windsor Terrace. The light is bright in the mornings and low and warm in the afternoons.

MATT. I think we should paint this room yellow.

PENELOPE. Yes.

MATT. What do you think?

PENELOPE. I like it here.

MATT. Me too.

PENELOPE. On the anniversary of your death Matt and I fight over where to go for dinner.

MATT. Just pick a place. I don't care.

PENELOPE. Well I don't care either.

MATT. Ughhhhhh! Fine, Thai food.

PENELOPE. Ehh. I don't know.

MATT. Well then *you* pick a place, Penelope!

PENELOPE. On the anniversary of your death Matt and I drink too much at a party and ride the subway home drunk.

MATT. *(half-asleep)* What stop are we?

PENELOPE. Not yet.

MATT. I drank too much.

PENELOPE. Me too.

MATT. I love you, Penelope.

PENELOPE. I love you.

On the anniversary of your death my sister takes the train up from DC to help me pick out a wedding dress. We find one with covered buttons all down the back. It's beautiful.

On the anniversary of your death I cut my finger while chopping garlic and have to get three stitches.

On the anniversary of your death there is a terrible thunderstorm and a tree falls on our block.

PENELOPE. *(cont.)* On the anniversary of your death Matt and I order pizza and play scrabble on the floor. We decide to go off the pill.

On the anniversary of your death I go out for a walk by myself for the first time since Eliza was born.

On the anniversary of your death she throws up all over the car on our way to visit my Dad in New Hampshire.

On the anniversary of your death I'm six months and exhausted.

On the anniversary of your death we're doing math homework and packing lunches,

MATT. we're worrying that she's shy,

PENELOPE. we're worrying he's unhappy,

MATT. we're picking up the babysitter,

PENELOPE. we're crying in the auditorium,

MATT. we're learning how to swim,

PENELOPE. we're making dinners

MATT. we're making breakfast

PENELOPE. we're making messes

MATT. we're getting through the weeks

PENELOPE. And at some point, a point I cannot identify, the memory of you shifts. It becomes sepia-toned and quiet.

(PENELOPE joins MATT; sitting somewhere; he is half asleep after a long day. It is very, very quiet – the feeling of late, late night. They hold hands.)

MATT. How are you doing?

PENELOPE. I'm okay.

MATT. I just remembered what today is.

PENELOPE. I know. I had forgotten until a couple hours ago when I was doing the dishes. And I was like, 'oh yeah.'

MATT. You're okay?

PENELOPE. I'm fine. How are you?

MATT. Tired.

PENELOPE. Yes.

MATT. I tried to read Nathaniel a story.

PENELOPE. Oh?

MATT. He told me he didn't need me to. "It's okay," he said, "I don't need it."

PENELOPE. Oh.

MATT. I wanted to say, "But I need it."

(They are quiet for a long moment.)

Time passes and passes and passes.

PENELOPE. Yes.

(She smiles and looks down at him, then stares out at their home. The sounds and light of night fade away.)

(end of play)

NAKED EYES

Dean Imperial

Naked Eyes was produced as part of the 37th Annual Samuel French Off Off Broadway Short Play Festival at the Beckett Theater at Theater Row in New York City on October 24, 2012. The cast was as follows:

MAN . . . . Chris Stack

WOMAN . . . . .Georgia Stauss

CHARACTERS

MAN – (mid 20's to mid 30's) Very handsome.

WOMAN – (mid 40's to late 50's) Somewhat attractive but haggard, worn-looking. Drunk. Very drunk.

SETTING

A bar. The actors face us, as if from the bartender's perspective.

ABOUT THE PLAYWRIGHT

Dean Imperial's plays include: *The Sit* (Soho Playhouse), *The Woman from 43* (Berkshire Playwright Lab with Kristen Johnston and Chris Stack), *The Heart Attack* (Soho Shorts), and *The Needle Through the Arm Trick* (Lesser America @ Theater for the New City). Other plays include *The Heartbreak Doctor & Mr. Breyerson & The Hypnotist*. He is the recipient of the 2010 Playwriting Award at The Southampton Writer's Conference.

(lights up)

(an almost empty bar)

(A very attractive but haggard **WOMAN** *[40's-50's] sits at the end of the bar. Drunk.)*

(very drunk)

(At the other end, a very attractive **MAN** *[30's] sits. He stares into his drink. It's his first.)*

(silence)

WOMAN. *(to* **MAN***)* Hey.

(silence

(She looks into her glass. Looks around.)

Hey.

(She sighs.)

(to "invisible" bartender, lifts her glass) Hey.

(She gestures for a refill. She swirls her finger in the air to suggesting another round.)

You from California?

(The **MAN** *doesn't respond. Lost in thought.)*

Hey.

MAN. *(as if woken up)* Yeah?

WOMAN. You from California?

(He stares at her.)

MAN. Am I from California? *(pause)* No. I'm not from California.

*(***MAN** *restores to his drink.)*

WOMAN. Oh. Okay.

MAN. *(into his drink)* Do I look like I'm from California?

WOMAN. Not anymore.

*(**MAN** looks at her.)*

MAN. Okay.

WOMAN. Whatever.

(He gets back to his drink.)

(silence)

*(The **WOMAN** lets out an enormous inebriated laugh to herself.)*

(shakes her head)

WOMAN. *(to herself)* Whooo. God...

*(**MAN** looks over. Shakes his head. Gets back to his drink.)*

*(**WOMAN**, suddenly, becomes solemn.)*

(She studies her drink.)

You an actor?

MAN. Me?

WOMAN. No. The invisible-guy-sitting-between-us. "Me." Yeah, you. Are you an actor?

MAN. Why?

WOMAN. Why? *(laughs to herself)* Actors are so funny. You're so touchy. "Why?" 'Cause you look like an actor. So what? You're a goodlookin' guy. You kind-of remind me of that guy, you know that guy, the guy in the movie...the movie about Henry Hill...

MAN. "Goodfellas?"

WOMAN. Yeeeeeaaah. And that other one where the guy cuts the top of his head off –

MAN. – *What?* –

WOMAN. – YOU KNOW the guy, I'm talking about –

MAN. – Ray Liotta –

WOMAN. – NO! No, no, no, no. No. Not him. Oh yeeeeaaaahhhh. YEAH. Yeah, him. Ray Liotta. You remind me of him.

(MAN sighs.)

MAN. Really.

WOMAN. Yeah. A younger one of him. Yeaaaahhhh…

(She laughs.)

(silence)

(becoming grave) I was an actress once.

(silence)

(into her glass) It didn't work out.

(MAN does not respond.)

(silence)

WOMAN. So, you are an actor, aren't you?

(MAN sighs.)

MAN. Why do you want to know that?

WOMAN. Boy, you have real attitude.

MAN. I have an attitude?

WOMAN. Yeah!

MAN. Just leave me alone –

WOMAN. – You're a real asshole-

MAN. – I'm an asshole? –

WOMAN. Oh, yeah…

MAN. Really?

WOMAN. You're a fuckin' asshole.

MAN. *You're* a fuckin' asshole.

WOMAN. I'm a fuckin' asshole? Why? Because I asked you a question?-

MAN. – No –

WOMAN. – A *little-bitty*-fuckin' question, I'm a fuckin' asshole –

MAN. – You're invading my space? –

WOMAN. – WHAT? –

MAN. – You're invading my space –

WOMAN. – YOUR SPACE… *I'm all the way over here –*

MAN. My concentration space.

WOMAN. Your *what?*

MAN. My concentration space.

WOMAN. Your *concentration space?*

MAN. Yeah.

WOMAN. *(beat, looks around)* What the fuck is "concentration space"?

MAN. Just leave me alone. That's what /concentration space is…

WOMAN. Concentration /space. Now I *know* you're an actor.

(silence)

Whatever.

(silence)

*(**WOMAN** laughs to herself. It's a private, hearty laugh.)*

WOMAN. I'm sorry.

(silence)

(no response)

Hey.

(looks over at him, waves) Hey!

(He looks at her, reluctantly.)

WOMAN. I'm sorry.

*(**MAN** sighs.)*

MAN. It's okay.

WOMAN. I'm just trying to make conversation. *(beat)* Sorry I fucked it all up.

MAN. It's okay. Don't worry about it.

*(**WOMAN** nods, drunkenly.)*

WOMAN. I'm really sorry.

*(**MAN** sighs.)*

MAN. It's fine. Don't worry about it.

(silence)

WOMAN. You know…I know who you are.

(silence)

MAN. What?

WOMAN. You know, I know who you are.

(pause)

*(**MAN** shakes his head.)*

MAN. Yeah? Who am I?

WOMAN. You're the son…of a really, really, really famous actor.

(pause)

*(**MAN** shakes his head.)*

And you. You're really good. You're really, really good. You did that movie set in Las Vegas – the one that Paul Verano wrote – and you had that scene as that guy – the dealer – when you catch the guy cheating and have him *(She makes an exaggerated thumb-ejection gesture.)* Eighty-sixed. Right? Am I right? come on…am I right?

MAN. Yeah.

WOMAN. Oh my god! You are SO good in that scene! Jesus Christ. SO good. Oh, shit. Shit. You were so good. You know who you reminded me of in that scene?

(pause)

MAN. *(reluctantly curious)* No. Who?

WOMAN. Oh, my God…what's his name…SHIT…the car chase…

MAN. Gene Hackman?

WOMAN. *(huge)* – NO! You're not a "Gene Hackman" – what's his name??? Sexy! Sexy! Cool – Ali McGraw… *(beat)* SHIT!

MAN. I don't know.

WOMAN. You're so young. Anyway, I can't think of it, him. It's fuckin' GREAT compliment. You reminded me of him.

MAN. Oh. Okay.

WOMAN. Your Dad's good, too. But you're good. I could
see it. You're good. You're real good.

(pause)

MAN. Thanks.

(silence)

WOMAN. Yeah, you know, I was an actress for a while.
But I just didn't have the – you know – the moxie or
whatever-it-is to do it or whatever-it-is. *(beat)* But my
grandmother…my grandmother hung in there for a
while. She did. She hung in there for a while. She was
an actress. *(nodding her head)* She was an actress. She
banged it out on Hollywood for a while, but she did
mostly extra-work. She was in a lot of the Columbia
Pictures from the 30's to early 40's. Her big story was
that she had an affair with Jimmy Stewart on the set of
"Mr. Smith Goes to Washington," she was an extra, I
mean, not really an affair-affair, but he had this thing
– Jimmy Stewart – had this thing where he'd like…pull
an extra off to the side – in this case, my grandmother,
Rose – and take her to the gaffers closet in between
takes and eat her pussy out.

*(**MAN** quickly looks up from his drink.)*

MAN. What?

WOMAN. Yeah. Apparently that was his thing.

MAN. Jimmy Stewart? No…

WOMAN. Oh, yeah. She said he was like a rabid dog. Wasn't
much of a stick man, though, never even pulled it out,
she never even saw it, seemed kinda weird but he just
used to get off going-down on extras. She said he liked
to do it because it would blow their mind. She said he
used to come up to her, put his hand on her shoulder
and say *(doing a half-way decent Jimmy Stewart impression)*
"Hey, Rosie…whattya say we take a little walkies and we
get Jimbo a little bite to eat…"

MAN. *(stunned)* WHAT?

WOMAN. Yep. *(nods drunkenly)* America's everyman. *(beat)* Whatever.

MAN. Jesus.

(silence)

I kinda wish I didn't know that.

WOMAN. So…what about you?

(pause)

MAN. What about me, what?

WOMAN. You gotta a gal?

(no response)

Or a fella?

*(**MAN** laughs.)*

MAN. No. No gal, right now.

WOMAN. A fella?

MAN. NO! *(beat)* That's not my thing.

WOMAN. Wanna come up to my hotel room?

(silence)

MAN. No.

(silence)

WOMAN. Why not?

MAN. Because…

(silence)

WOMAN. You know, I know why you're here.

MAN. *(laughs, shakes his head)* Why? Why am I here?

WOMAN. You're here because you're in town shooting that movie. That independent movie. "Naked Eyes." Right? That's the name of it, right? "Naked Eyes?"

MAN. Yeah. That's the name of it.

WOMAN. It's about the little blind kid who's clairvoyant and his parents. He sees the murder of the woman across the street.

MAN. Yeah. *(beat)* How'd you know that?

WOMAN. Because I wrote it.

(silence)

MAN. No you didn't.

*(**WOMAN** nods her head. Lifts her glass up to him.)*

You're Ellen Randolph?

WOMAN. Wanna look at my I.D.?

(silence)

MAN. Yeah. *(laughs)* I do.

*(**WOMAN** drunkenly looks for her purse, finds her wallet, opens it, and shows it to him.)*

(He looks.)

MAN. Wow. *(beat)* You're Ellen Randolph.

(She nods drunkenly.)

(pause)

It's a good script.

WOMAN. Thanks.

MAN. No, it's a really good script. It's really excellent. I love it. I'm not just saying that. I love what it has to say.

*(The **WOMAN** laughs.)*

WOMAN. "What it has to say?"

MAN. Yeah.

WOMAN. You're such an actor.

MAN. No, seriously. It's one of the best scripts I've ever read. Ever. I wanted to do it so badly. Even the part of the father – that's not that the most exciting role – I'm still really proud to be in it.

WOMAN. You don't like the role of the father?

MAN. No, it's not that, what I'm saying is that – the father may not be the showiest role, but – but, I'm still really proud to be in such an excellent screenplay…even though…the role…isn't…doesn't…have as much to do…as say…the detective…or…the mother…or the neighbor.

WOMAN. Uh-huh.

(*pause*)

MAN. That's all I'm saying.

(WOMAN *nods her head. Takes a drink.*)

I'm sorry about before.

WOMAN. It's fine. (*beat*) I was fuckin' with you. (*beat*) I should have identified myself.

MAN. Yeah. I'm sorry.

WOMAN. It's funny how a little bitty piece of information can change you're whole perspective on somebody.

MAN. Yeah. It's true. (*beat*) That's definitely true.

(*pause*)

WOMAN. So, now you wanna fuck me?

MAN. What?

WOMAN. You wanna come up to my hotel room and fuck me now?

(*pause*)

(MAN *laughs. Shakes his head.*)

MAN. I...I don't...I don't...do you really *want* that?

(*She nods her head.*)

I don't think it's a good idea.

WOMAN. Come on.

MAN. Come on, what?

WOMAN. Fuck the writer.

MAN. What?

WOMAN. Fuck the writer!

MAN. Oh, my god.

WOMAN. You don't want to fuck the writer?

MAN. What? No, it's not that.

WOMAN. Come on! I need it!

MAN. No! I don't want to!

(*silence*)

(**WOMAN** *goes dark, suddenly. She puts her face in her hand.*)

(*She begins sobbing.*)

(*The* **MAN** *stares into his drink.*)

(*silence*)

MAN. (*cont.*) Hey.

(*She does not respond.*)

Hey.

(**WOMAN** *looks up from her sobbing.*)

I'm sorry.

WOMAN. (*quiety*) It's alright.

MAN. And I lied before. I *am* from California.

WOMAN. (*laughs*) Yeah. I know. (*beat*) Christ. (*beat*) You actors are so touchy.

MAN. I'm touchy? (*shakes his head*) What about writers?

WOMAN. Writers aren't touchy. Actors are touchy.

MAN. (*laughs*) Then what are writers?

(*pause*)

WOMAN. (*gravely serious*) Suicidal.

(*silence*)

MAN. You want another drink?

WOMAN. You're gonna buy me a drink?

MAN. Yeah. (*beat*) And maybe…maybe…I'll come up to your room and hang out. Just…hang out.

(**WOMAN** *begins nodding her head.*)

WOMAN. Maybe I can get a little Jimmy Stewart action?

MAN. Maybe. *Maybe*…we'll see.

(*pause*)

WOMAN. Alright.

(*pause*)

(**WOMAN** *lets out a huge laugh.*)

MAN. What? *(beat)* What?

WOMAN. Steve McQueen. That's who you remind me of. Steve McQueen. "Bullet." The car chase. "Bullet."

MAN. Oh. *(thinks about it)* Okay. That's cool. *(beat)* Thanks.

(She stares at him. Vacant.)

WOMAN. Yeah. *(Beat. She tosses back the rest of her drink.)* Whatever.

(lights out)

(end of play)

FORGETTING TO REMEMBER

Greg Kalleres

Forgetting to Remember was produced as part of the 37th Annual Samuel French Off Off Broadway Short Play Festival at the Beckett Theater at Theater Row in New York City on October 25, 2012. It was directed by Ken Kalssar. The cast was as follows:

WILLA . . . . Glory Gallo
CANICE . . . . Marc Garber
MAX . . . . Jonathan Monk

CHARACTERS

CANICE
WILLA
MAX

ABOUT THE PLAYWRIGHT

Greg Kalleres' plays have been produced all over the country. He received the Certificate of Excellence from the Kennedy Center, is a two-time finalist for the Lila Acheson American Playwrights Program at Juilliard, and a two-time finalist for Aurora Theatre Company's Global Age Project. He won Best Play two consecutive years at the Turnip 15-Minute Play Festival, the Jury Prize and Audience Favorite Award at Fusion Theatre Company's one act play festival, and was fortunate enough to be selected for the Samuel French Off Off Broadway Festival last year for his play, *Hiding From Adults*.

(lights up on a bedroom, late at night)

*(**CANICE** gets out of bed and shuffles to the bathroom.)*

(Toilet flushes. Water runs.)

(He comes back out and stops when he sees...a strange woman in his bed.)

(Shocked, he approaches her slowly, cautiously. He pokes her. He pulls off the covers and looks at her. She pulls the covers back up.)

(He then frantically looks around the room for clues. Under the bed, in the closet, rummaging through her clothes.)

*(Meanwhile, the woman, **WILLA**, wakes up and watches him, half asleep.)*

WILLA. What are you doing?

CANICE. *(startled)* Huh?!

WILLA. Come back to bed.

> *(**WILLA** crashes back onto the pillow as **CANICE** stands frozen, staring at her.)*
>
> *(A moment passes.)*
>
> *(She sits up again, annoyed.)*

WILLA. *What?!*

CANICE. Did we...you know...?

WILLA. Yeah, I turned it off last night.

CANICE. No! Did we...? I mean, you know, last night? Together?

WILLA. What the hell are you talking about?

CANICE. I don't know how much I drank last night. I don't remember. It must have been a lot, I don't know. But please tell me that you and I didn't...do it.

WILLA. Do it??

CANICE. *(trying to be quiet)* Have sex!

WILLA. *(sardonic)* Us? Yeah, right.

(She goes back to bed.)

CANICE. No! You can't go back to sleep! We have to get you out of here!

*(**CANICE** tries to get her out of bed.)*

WILLA. Hey! What are you – ?

CANICE. C'mon, before my wife sees you!

WILLA. Your *what?!*

CANICE. C'mon! We gotta get you....here!

(He tries putting a shirt on her.)

WILLA. Stop!

CANICE. C'mon! You can go out the window!

WILLA. Canice, stop!

CANICE. Look, if she finds you here, I'm dead!

WILLA. Are you dreaming?! You're fucking dreaming!

CANICE. SHHHH! Look, I don't want to hurt your feelings. I'm sure you're a very nice person, really! And very, you know, attractive – in your way! But I have no idea who you are or how you got here! I just want you out before Willa comes back. Now, I think we can get you through the window – although, you're a little big.

WILLA. Canice!

CANICE. Maybe you could suck in a little?

WILLA. Canny! Wake up!

(This stops him.)

CANICE. You just called me Canny.

WILLA. Yes, I called you Canny.

*(**CANICE** realizes something)*

CANICE. You bitch, what have you done with my wife? Where's the baby?!

*(**WILLA** gets up and walks to the bathroom.)*

CANICE. Is this about money? Blackmail? Did you drug me last night? Is that how –

(She emerges with a glass of water and throws it on his face.)

WILLA. I am your wife! We've been married for twenty-six years! Now wake the fuck up so we can go back to sleep!

(pause)

CANICE. I don't know what you want but I will not allow one night of depraved sex with some chunky, middle-aged bar fly to ruin my marriage with Willa!

WILLA. I am Willa!!

CANICE. *(still not getting it)* You're name is Willa too.

WILLA. I am Willa!! I am the only Willa you know! The Willa you married!

CANICE. I've never seen you before in my life.

WILLA. Canice stop this! You're scaring me.

CANICE. You stop! Stop trying to be my wife!

WILLA. I'm calling the doctor!

CANICE. I'm calling the police!

WILLA. Stop, you need a doctor!

CANICE. Give me the phone!

(They fight over the phone.)

(MAX, twenty-five, shuffles in.)

MAX. Guys, could you like keep it down.

(CANICE jumps.)

CANICE. Who the hell are you?!

MAX. Dad, you okay?

CANICE. Dad??

WILLA. I'm calling the doctor.

CANICE. Who the hell is he calling *Dad*?

WILLA. Your father's having a stroke, will you help me?

MAX. Do what?

WILLA. I don't know; make sure he doesn't swallow his tongue!

MAX. Why would he swallow his tongue?

WILLA. I don't know! Just do something!

(**WILLA** *dials as* **MAX** *walks over to* **CANICE** *and sticks his fingers in his mouth.*)

CANICE. What are you doing?

MAX. Mom doesn't want you to swallow you're tongue.

CANICE. Why would I swallow my tongue?

MAX. I don't know, it was mom's idea.

(**CANICE** *grabs the phone and hangs it up.*)

CANICE. *(testing)* Where did we go for our honeymoon?

WILLA. Miami!

CANICE. The whole time?!

WILLA. No, then we went to the Keys! You got bit by a jellyfish. We made love on the balcony of our suite and you pulled your back out.

MAX. Aw, guys, please!

WILLA. MAX! Shut, up!

CANICE. Max??

MAX. Yeah.

CANICE. *Max??*

MAX. WHAT?

CANICE. *Little Maxy??*

WILLA. That's little Maxy! He's twenty-five, remember? He grew up! Well, he got taller, anyway.

CANICE. Wait, wait…

WILLA. What did you eat last night?

CANICE. Willa and I had left over pork chops.

WILLA. And what does "Willa" look like?

CANICE. She…looks…like you, I guess. I mean…she has your eyes, and your…hair, I suppose. But…she's beautiful.

WILLA. It's four in the morning; what to you want?

MAX. Maybe he got into my stash.

WILLA. Max, not now!

CANICE. *(testing again)* What's your mother's name?

WILLA. Tammie!

CANICE. What's my mothers name?

WILLA. Doris!

CANICE. What shape is the birthmark on your back?

WILLA. I don't have a birthmark on my back.

CANICE. DAMN!!

WILLA. Did you get into Max's stash?

> (**CANICE** *walks over to* **MAX** *and touches his face, looks into his eyes; examining.*)

CANICE. Max?

MAX. Uh, Mom?

CANICE. Maxy.

MAX. It's gonna be alright, Dad.

CANICE. Stop calling me Dad! You can't even speak yet! *(to* **WILLA***)* And you! This can't be you. You look so…sad! So ancient.

WILLA. And you haven't had a sustainable erection in two years – welcome to the club!

MAX. Aw, dude…

CANICE. What?? Two years!

WILLA. And three days to be exact.

CANICE. That can't be! I'm a sustainer. I sustain.

MAX. Dad, please…

WILLA. Not anymore you don't.

CANICE. What are you talking about? The other night!

WILLA. The other…?! Will you go look at yourself for Christ sake!

> (**CANICE** *runs to the bathroom. They wait.*)

CANICE. *(offstage)* Holy shit!! Mother, son of bitch!!!! What the – what is *that?!* When did – ???

(He comes out.)

CANICE. What happened to me?

WILLA. You got old.

CANICE. Old! No. We, no, we weren't gonna get old, remember?

WILLA. *(humoring him)* Yeah.

MAX. Dude this is fucking weird.

CANICE. And you! Max! I just changed your diapers.

MAX. It's possible; I get a little too drunk sometimes.

(CANICE looks at WILLA.)

CANICE. We have such plans for him. Don't we?

WILLA. We did. Yeah.

CANICE. What happened?

MAX. When?

CANICE. With your life. What have you done?

MAX. Uh…?

CANICE. We were gonna sign you up for piano lessons. Do you, do you play?

MAX. Piano? No.

CANICE. Well. What do you do?

MAX. Yeah, I'm not following you.

WILLA. He means, with your life, what do you do? The answer is nothing!

MAX. Oh. Yeah. Pretty much.

CANICE. But we talked about this. We talked just yesterday about the kind of man he would be.

MAX. You did?

CANICE. YES!

MAX. What did you come up with?

CANICE. Smart. Compassionate. Talented. We imagined something in politics, medicine, maybe the arts!

MAX. Oh! Well, kind of! I'm gay!

CANICE. What?!

MAX. What, no good?

CANICE. I don't understand...

WILLA. What was the last thing you remember?

CANICE. Having a sustainable erection!

MAX. Dad, no one wants to hear about your sustainable erection!

CANICE. That's easy for you to say, you gay bastard – you're twenty-five! You're probably sustaining all over the place!

WILLA. Everyone stop saying sustain!! Now think. What do you remember?

(pause)

CANICE. I don't know. You and I at the kitchen table... eating left over pork chops your Mom had left in our freezer. Little Maxy in his crib. Just next to us. So small. So much life to live. And you...so beautiful. So...young. We had so many plans. Did we do any of them?

WILLA. Sure. Some.

CANICE. Like which?

WILLA. I had my tubes tied like you wanted.

CANICE. What else?

WILLA. You wanted to buy your mother a house so we could have the house to ourselves.

CANICE. And we did that?

WILLA. Well, she died.

CANICE. She did?? When?

WILLA. Ten years ago.

CANICE. Oh god.

MAX. Does this mean you don't remember me failing out of college?

CANICE. You failed out of college?!

MAX. SHIT! Stupid!

CANICE. What about me? I wanted to be a writer. Did I do it? Did I...succeed?

MAX. *(giggling)* Sure, Dad. You're a writer.

CANICE. What does that mean? What does he mean?

WILLA. He means...we had to make sacrifices and you had to take a steadier job. You write...copy for a toilet paper company.

CANICE. Toilet paper?

MAX. You're the best at your company.

CANICE. I think I'm gonna throw up.

WILLA. Look, we all have plans, you know, but sometimes priorities switch. Things change. Okay? You adapt. You don't just pretend none of it happened!

(pause)

CANICE. And then I woke up. And there you were. Old. Me. Old. You. Gay.

MAX. Bi.

CANICE. Really?

MAX. Sometimes.

CANICE. Sometimes bi?

MAX. Depends on how much energy I have.

CANICE. I don't even know what that means!

WILLA. Max, just shut up.

MAX. That's sounds familiar.

WILLA. Please, not now.

MAX. Don't like what he's saying, shut him up.

WILLA. Alright...

MAX. That's the way it's always been, hasn't it, Mom?

WILLA. No.

MAX. No?

CANICE. Has it?

WILLA. No.

MAX. Yes.

WILLA. Shut up!

MAX. See?

WILLA. Max, your father might have a tumor in his cerebellum! Now is not the time!

CANICE. Is this how we talk to each other?

WILLA. Oh, Jesus! What is this, *A Christmas Carol?!*

CANICE. Max! Did we ever…play catch in the back yard? I always wanted to do that.

MAX. Yeah, Dad, we played catch sometimes.

CANICE. Did you have fun?

MAX. Yeah, actually. I did.

CANICE. So…then what? What made you so…?

MAX. Gay?

CANICE. Depressed.

MAX. I don't know. I don't remember.

WILLA. Not you too.

CANICE. And you. When did you get like this?

WILLA. You say I'm old one more time…

CANICE. So angry! So…

MAX. Intolerant?

CANICE. Is she?

MAX. Yes.

WILLA. I am not!

MAX. Mom, when I told you I was gay you pretended I said I was "Dave."

WILLA. You mumble.

MAX. It doesn't even rhyme! And for an entire year you called me Dave so you wouldn't have to deal with it. Finally Dad said… "hey, you know, he didn't say his name was Dave, he said he was gay!"

WILLA. I don't remember any of this.

CANICE. What about me? What was I like? Am I like?

MAX. You're…fine.

CANICE. Fine?

MAX. In the beginning. I mean...I don't know...

WILLA. I really don't remember what you're talking about?

CANICE. What Maxy? Tell me.

MAX. In the beginning you guys were...happy. I guess. We were all pretty happy. And as the years went on you seemed to just separate.

CANICE. Us?

MAX. You both from each other. You both from me. You stopped talking. You stopped acknowledging me. It was like time stopped. Like we were all waiting for the laundry to be done. And we all just...passed the time.

CANICE. How?

MAX. You guys worked. I fucked up. Over and over. Maybe trying to disrupt the spin cycle.

(**WILLA** *now sits, depressed*)

Playing catch in the back yard? That's the last good memory I have.

WILLA. I don't remember. Any of this.

MAX. Maybe that's for the best.

CANICE. No! No, I want to remember! Goddamnit! I don't like this. I woke up one day to find that my family depresses the living shit out of me. I'm failure as a husband, as a father, as a man...

MAX. And there's whole erection thing.

CANICE. Yes! Thank you! I was grouping that in with everything else! *(beat)* But this is what I got. Isn't it? And I used to love you. Very much. I remember that. And you loved me.

(pause)

WILLA. Yes.

CANICE. Well?

WILLA. I'm scared suddenly.

CANICE. Me too.

WILLA. I don't want to go back to sleep.

CANICE. We won't. We wont ever again.

*(**CANICE** sits with his wife and holds her hand.)*

CANICE. Max? Come here.

*(**MAX** walks to his family. They all sit on the bed.)*

We'll just sit here until morning. We'll just sit, awake, so that we miss nothing.

WILLA. How do we stay awake?

MAX. I actually have something that might help.

CANICE. No! No. We'll just talk. All night. So that we hear the change in our voices and see the lines grow on our faces. We'll talk until we remember what we forgot to remember. We'll start over if we have to. Okay?

(pause)

Now, Max…what do you want to be when you grow up?

(lights out)

(end of play)

WOLF PLAY

Claire Kiechel

"And now my fur has turned to skin,
I've been quickly ushered in
To a world that, I confess, I do not know
But I still dream of running careless through the snow."
                                                    — Blitzen Trapper

Wolf Play was produced as part of the 37th Annual Samuel French Off Off Broadway Short Play Festival at the Beckett Theater at Theater Row in New York City on October 27, 2012. The cast was as follows:

MATTHEW . . . . Joe Curnutte

JULIET . . . . Rebecca Hirota

CHARACTERS

MATTHEW
JULIET

ABOUT THE PLAYWRIGHT

Claire Kiechel has been developing *Norway* at the Orchard Project, as well as a piece inspired by Anne Sexton's poetry with Helikon Rep, and her graduate thesis play set in the 1870s. Other plays include: *Whale Song Or: Learning to Live with Mobyphobia* (FringeNYC 2011); *Luxembourg* (Lunar Energy Productions & AntiMatter Collective); *Kissing Ronald Reagan: A Burlesque Tragedy, Radical Methods For Radical Heartbreak*, and her adaptation of the Odyssey, *Lethe* (New School for Drama). Claire is getting her MFA in playwriting at the New School for Drama and is a member of the Dramatists Guild. www.clairekiechel.com

(MATTHEW has a pile of rope that he is sorting and cutting. JULIET hugs him from behind.)

JULIET. Whatcha doing?

MATTHEW. You're very funny.

JULIET. Well, you're very sweaty.

MATTHEW. I'm working!

JULIET. Mmm.

(She kisses him.)

Salty.

MATTHEW. Okay, alright, let me finish.

(He continues cutting the rope.)

(JULIET picks up a piece of the rope he's holding, tugs at it.)

JULIET. You know it's been ten years?

MATTHEW. Only ten? Feels longer.

JULIET. Ten years tonight actually. Happy anniversary to me.

MATTHEW. Happy anniversary to us. I'm proud of you.

JULIET. Thanks.

MATTHEW. Naomi asleep?

JULIET. She's in bed, but she says she's too excited for the Running to sleep.

MATTHEW. I'll talk to her.

JULIET. She won't listen to me.

MATTHEW. You just have to know what to threaten her with.

JULIET. I try! She never believes me.

MATTHEW. And then, you have to follow through. All done.

(He puts down the rope, gestures to the chair.)

JULIET. It's not time yet.

MATTHEW. Pretty close.

JULIET. I was thinking…what if we didn't tonight?

MATTHEW. Honey.

JULIET. Don't say no before you hear me out.

MATTHEW. I'm listening.

JULIET. I woke up this morning, and I thought, I don't need this anymore. It was like…something had lifted inside of me.

MATTHEW. Uh huh.

(He picks up the rope.)

JULIET. You are so not listening to me!

MATTHEW. You try to talk your way out of this every time. Don't say you don't.

JULIET. But, it's different tonight. It just feels like any other Saturday.

MATTHEW. It's getting late, sweetie.

JULIET. Why don't I make us martinis? We can watch TV, listen to some records.

MATTHEW. It's better to be safe than sorry.

JULIET. But how we will ever know unless you trust me?

MATTHEW. It's not that I don't trust you.

JULIET. Feels like that.

MATTHEW. Three years ago you kicked me in the nuts trying to escape.

JULIET. That was an accident! You always bring that up.

MATTHEW. I want you to remember what you get like.

JULIET. I'm better now. I got the "most well-adjusted award" in Group.

MATTHEW. Didn't someone in your group just get caught eating a *cat?*

JULIET. A pet rabbit. And that wasn't Gary's fault, it was just instinct.

MATTHEW. Instinct. Right. Get in the chair, Juliet.

JULIET. Please. Matt. I was good last year! And this year, it doesn't even smell like a Running.

MATTHEW. Oh, it doesn't?

JULIET. I would never ask unless I thought it was safe.

MATTHEW. Alright. Let's compromise. Tonight, I'll tie you a little looser, and if you don't freak out or kick me in my special place, then...next year we'll try something else.

JULIET. I want to try tonight.

MATTHEW. *(gestures to the chair or says "Chair")*

JULIET. No.

> **(MATTHEW** *lunges at her and wrangles her into the chair.)*

MATTHEW. You always want to make me work for it.

JULIET. This is so stupid.

MATTHEW. It's stupid to want my wife in the morning?

JULIET. You're so insecure.

MATTHEW. Insecure? How many ex-runners went back last year?

JULIET. I don't know. Two?

MATTHEW. That's two too many.

JULIET. But Bree and Freddy never fully adapted. I'm not like them.

MATTHEW. Once a runner, always a runner, isn't that what your Group leader says? It's something inside of you you'll always have to control.

JULIET. I fucking control myself every day.

> *(He kisses her.)*

MATTHEW. Calm down.

> *(He pets her for a second.)*
>
> *(She quiets.)*

JULIET. Naomi asked me why I couldn't read with her tonight.

MATTHEW. You didn't tell her?

JULIET. No, because I controlled myself! And cause I didn't know – how.

MATTHEW. When she gets older, we'll let her know about you.

JULIET. We should have done it this year.

MATTHEW. She's not ready.

JULIET. I was her age when I ran.

MATTHEW. That's not going to happen to her.

JULIET. She said that they had the assembly today. PowerPoint and everything – it was different back in my day.

MATTHEW. They think some slideshow is going to make it less dangerous?

JULIET. I guess every town has its thing.

MATTHEW. They shouldn't be talking to the kids about it, that's the parents' job. All done.

(He finishes tying her up.)

JULIET. I look like a turkey dinner.

MATTHEW. You mean you look delicious.

JULIET. Are you going to make me stay like this all night?

MATTHEW. Sooner you accept it, the better you'll feel.

(He checks his watch.)

Almost time.

JULIET. I can't tell.

(He goes to a box of records.)

MATTHEW. What do you want to listen to?

JULIET. My wrist hurts.

MATTHEW. Cole Porter? Frank Sinatra?

JULIET. You've tied my wrist too tight.

MATTHEW. Django Reinhardt?

JULIET. Matt! It really hurts.

MATTHEW. Fine.

(He goes over to her and loosens it.)

MATTHEW. That better?

JULIET. Much. Can you scratch my nose?

(He does.)

MATTHEW. Right there? The nook? You're very cute.

JULIET. I'd be much cuter if you untied me.

(a single howl)

(They both stiffen.)

MATTHEW. Here we go.

(He goes back to the record box, looks through them. The following lines overlap.)

MATTHEW. /What did you say you wanted to listen to?

JULIET. /When you're a Runner, you don't remember things until you have to.

*(**MATTHEW** holds up an album.)*

MATTHEW. /Beach Boys the wrong mood?

JULIET. /When you're hungry, you remember where to hunt. When you're thirsty, you remember where to drink.

MATTHEW. /Beatles. More Beatles. The Cure.

JULIET. /When you're scared you remember how to run.

MATTHEW. Stop.

JULIET. What?

MATTHEW. You know I don't like you talking like that.

JULIET. Like what?

MATTHEW. Romanticizing the whole thing.

JULIET. I'm not doing that.

MATTHEW. Whenever it starts, you go into this memory place.

JULIET. I do not.

MATTHEW. You do too!

JULIET. Okay, cranky, are you the one tied up in the garage?

MATTHEW. I've had a hard day too, you know? Having to listen to the newscasters all day? "Remember folks, tonight is the Running, lock up your puppies and your wives, and stay indoors." I mean, if it's so bad, if it's so dangerous, why doesn't the town put a stop to it?

JULIET. What do you mean?

MATTHEW. I don't know.

JULIET. You mean use violence?

MATTHEW. No, but why do you think I keep a gun around? Eventually one of the Runners is going to go berserk and somebody's going to get hurt.

JULIET. We just need to stay out of their way once a year.

MATTHEW. But we still lose people every year. I mean, yeah, it's their decision to run, but if I were the mayor, I would –

JULIET. You'd what?

MATTHEW. I'd get put a stop to it, make them leave. Think of how much real estate values would go up.

JULIET. Those are our friends out there.

MATTHEW. They were our friends. And now they're not.

JULIET. Okay, Matt.

MATTHEW. Don't okay Matt me. You know what Barry at work said yesterday? He said, "Your wife's an ex-runner, right?" Like it was something okay to talk about.

JULIET. Who cares what Barry/ thinks –

MATTHEW. /And then he says, "I hear those ex-Runners get extra frisky around this time, let me know if you need me to come over and give you a hand." What am I supposed to say to that?

JULIET. Barry's a child.

MATTHEW. I shouldn't have to worry about this shit. It's not normal.

JULIET. I'm sorry I'm not normal.

MATTHEW. That's not what I mean.

JULIET. I'm sorry you have to *deal* with me.

MATTHEW. I wasn't saying that!

(*a wolf howl as they listen*)

JULIET. My wrist still hurts, can you loosen it?

MATTHEW. Yeah. You know I don't want to hurt you.

(He loosens it.)

JULIET. I've always liked our story.

MATTHEW. It's not that I don't like it.

JULIET. I saw you and I knew I wanted you.

MATTHEW. Oh come on.

JULIET. You were very sexy.

MATTHEW. Really? Just lying there with a twisted ankle?

JULIET. Very cute and helpless.

MATTHEW. I was terrified. You were terrifying.

JULIET. I thought you liked the way I looked.

MATTHEW. Naked, muddy, sticks in your hair. Yeah, it was a good look for you.

JULIET. You gave me a cookie. That Oreo?

MATTHEW. I didn't want you to eat me.

JULIET. One bite, and wooosh, I remembered. Oreos in milk. And my mother. Everything came back.

MATTHEW. And I was there.

JULIET. And you were there and when I saw you, I remembered what I wanted.

MATTHEW. Yeah?

JULIET. A man. A very strong and sexy man.

MATTHEW. Are you trying to flirt your way out of this?

JULIET. Maybe.

(She squirms sexily.)

MATTHEW. I'm not kissing you. I know where that leads.

JULIET. Tell me where it leads. I just want you.

(a wolf howl)

MATTHEW. Later you can have me all you want.

JULIET. I need you now.

MATTHEW. Stop.

JULIET. Touch me.

MATTHEW. No.

JULIET. God, you are so annoying.

(a howl)

(**JULIET** *stiffens.*)

JULIET. *(cont.)* It's Greta.

MATTHEW. It sounded closer, didn't it?

JULIET. When she was my pack leader,/she used to do this ritual –

MATTHEW. /Seems early for them to be this close.

(a crashing sound)

What was that?

JULIET. I don't know.

MATTHEW. You think – Naomi? I'm going to go see if she's in bed.

(**MATTHEW** *exits quickly, leaving* **JULIET** *alone.*)

(She looks around, and then begins to bite through the ropes of her wrists.)

(She undoes one and then undoes the other. She gets it off, when she hears **MATTHEW** *approaching. She quickly arranges the ropes so that it looks like they are still secure.)*

(**MATTHEW** *enters.*)

She's okay. I locked her door.

JULIET. Is she scared? I can go and cuddle with her.

MATTHEW. No. You don't want her to see you like this.

(two wolf howls)

JULIET. There's a new one with Greta. A male.

MATTHEW. Don't talk like that.

JULIET. You want to know what they're saying?

MATTHEW. Not really.

(**MATTHEW** *goes back over to the box of records.*)

How about the Big Bopper?

JULIET. What makes you not trust me?

MATTHEW. I do trust you.

JULIET. Then let me out.

MATTHEW. Soundtrack to *Cabaret?* You like that one.

(*He continues flipping through the records.*)

JULIET. Please Matt. I do all these things for you every day. Mother things. Wife things. I just want to do something for myself.

MATTHEW. Do what? You mean, run? You're admitting you want to run?

JULIET. I just want to be trusted. Ten years? Don't I get any credit? I've been very good, haven't I?

MATTHEW. Mostly.

JULIET. Mostly?

MATTHEW. You want to sleep with everyone. Lloyd. Colin. Whenever I bring a man over, I can smell it on you.

JULIET. I don't do anything!

MATTHEW. But you want to. I can tell. It's getting worse lately, it's like you're stifling something.

JULIET. I don't even flirt.

MATTHEW. Yes you do. Don't lie.

JULIET. I'm not allowed to talk to people now?

MATTHEW. Not if you're going to look at them that way.

JULIET. What way?

MATTHEW. Other people's wives don't look at men like that.

(*a realization*)

JULIET. That's what this is about.

MATTHEW. Admit it. You think about it.

JULIET. Everybody thinks about it.

MATTHEW. I don't. I only think about you.

JULIET. I can't help that. What do you want from me?

MATTHEW. I don't want you to leave me.

JULIET. I wasn't planning on it. But when you start accusing me/ of

MATTHEW. It's not an accusation if it's true.

JULIET. Untie me.

MATTHEW. I can't.

JULIET. I am done with this, Matt. And, if I want to go running tonight, I will. Because I am not your prisoner.

(JULIET rips the ropes off her wrists and begins to untie her ankles.)

MATTHEW. No. No.

(MATTHEW tackles and chokes her.)

(a refrain, as long as it needs to be) I'm sorry, I'm sorry, I'm sorry...

(He lets go of her neck.)

(She struggles for air while he ties her up.)

(He pulls her in, makes a final knot.)

(She screams and then begins to howl.)

(He puts his hand over her mouth. She bites him.)

Ow.

(She continues to howl until he finally gets her quiet with his hand.)

JULIET. Don't touch me.

MATTHEW. Then stop making so much noise.

(two howls, closer and louder)

JULIET. They're coming. You want to know what I said?

MATTHEW. No.

JULIET. I said, Help. He's got me. I'm one of yours. They're on their way.

MATTHEW. Here?

JULIET. I would make sure the door is locked.

MATTHEW. Tell them to go back. Tell them you're fine.

JULIET. They always know when you're lying.

MATTHEW. You are fine.

(Two howls get louder, closer.)

JULIET. Greta's worried. She's coming.

MATTHEW. Is this some kind of game for you? You're going to get us killed.

JULIET. I'll make it right. You just need to untie me.

MATTHEW. And if I do?

JULIET. I'll run out and greet them. I'll tell them I'm fine. I'll be back tomorrow.

MATTHEW. You won't come back.

JULIET. Trust me.

(a lone howl)

He's coming too.

MATTHEW. Who?

JULIET. The new male. He's on his way with Greta.

MATTHEW. You tell him to go back or else.

JULIET. Or else what?

MATTHEW. You're not going with Greta. You're not going with some new male.

JULIET. *(a refrain, simultaneous with MATTHEW's words)* Let me out. Let me out. Let me out. Let me out.

MATTHEW. /We are happy, and we love each other and everything is fine. Except for this one thing. We can get through this.

JULIET. I am tired of having to remember what I can or cannot do, what I can or cannot say. I just want to be me for one fucking night.

MATTHEW. It won't be just one night.

JULIET. Then you better be ready to keep me tied up forever.

MATTHEW. Don't say that.

(the howls are right outside.)

JULIET. They're here.

MATTHEW. You shouldn't have brought them here.

JULIET. They'll get in. Let me out.

MATTHEW. Just shut up for a minute.

(She starts to howl.)

(He tapes her mouth shut. She is silent.)

(concerned howls outside)

(**MATTHEW** *goes to the drawer, pulls out a revolver.*)

(He exits.)

(Offstage, two gunshots ring out. A yelp. Silence.)

(**JULIET** *whimpers.*)

(**MATTHEW** *walks across the stage with his gun, exits towards Naomi's room.*)

MATTHEW. *(offstage)* It's okay. We're all okay. We're just playing a game out here. I'll be in in a minute.

(He re-enters, puts the gun down.)

(He puts on a record. Some music. Low. Something like Billie Holiday's "They Can't Take That Away From Me".*)

You like this right? Yeah, this is good. *(he hums the tune)* I'm not going to hurt you. I would never hurt you. I knew the first time I saw you in the woods that I was always going to take care of you. Remember that Oreo? You just gobbled it right out of my hands. And then you smelled me, and you liked what you smelled. Look at me. I saw those eyes and I knew you wanted me like I wanted you. And I named you Juliet. Because you are my Juliet. You're my pretty girl. I'll make you breakfast in bed tomorrow. Naomi will help, so you won't have to do anything. Doesn't that sound good? I just want you to make you feel good.

(end of play)

---

* See Music Use Note on page 3

MISSED CONNECTION

Catya McMullen

Missed Connection was originally produced as a part of the UNC Chapel Hill Department of Dramatic Art Undergraduate Production's 24 Hour Play Festival in 2011. It was directed by Amelia Sciandra. The cast was as follows:

FLYNN . . . . .Jeb Brinkley
RAE . . . . .Chessa Rich

CHARACTERS

FLYNN – Funny boy with an overt appreciation of beauty. A sucker for tiny, hip delicate flowers, something that has gotten him into trouble in the past.

RAE – Smart ass girl. Lonely.

PLAYWRIGHT'S NOTE

BOY and **GIRL** should be played by the actors playing **RAE** and **FLYNN**

SETTING

Various locations at people's computers. And then a park bench in Carrboro, North Carolina.

TIME

Now.

ABOUT THE PLAYWRIGHT

Over her last year in New York, Catya has written and received sold-out readings of multiple plays by a number of companies including *Rubber Ducks and Sunsets*, *The Collective* with Ground UP Productions, and *When Predator Dies* with The Shelter. She is a 2011 graduate of UNC Chapel Hill, where *Missed Connection* was produced as a part of their Department of Dramatic Art's first annual 24 Hour Play Festival, and where her play *The Collective* received its first production.

SCENE 1

(There are two chairs, back to back, one facing the back of the stage, one facing the audience. **BOY** *and* **GIRL** *should swap seats as they change characters. Character changes can be marked by costume changes, adding a t-shirt or scarf or hat etc. when appropriate.)*

BOY. M4M 36 Fairfax

You, the beefcake in the pink polo who happened to be the only man without male pattern baldness at seven am in the locker room at the YMCA. Your stretching was thorough and diligent this morning. Thank you.

GIRL. W4W 25 Bakersfield

You, the girl making loud fart jokes in the Harris Teeter on Thursday night: I hated you until I turned the corner and saw you next to the frozen pizzas. I think you're beautiful. Let's go drinking and see what happens.

BOY. M4W, 42 Birmingham

Dear girl in the Bojangles eating a biscuit with your Momma, when you dropped your bible, I saw your thong.

GIRL. W4M 21 Washington DC

To the schwastey boy in the squid costume next to the chip bowl at the "under the sea" themed Sig Beta Pi mixer; thank you for smiling at me. I thought you were going to talk to me, but I guess you were too busy barfing in your fraternity brother's lobster helmet to say hi. Next time, try moderation. I was lonely and you would've gotten laid.

*(***FLYNN*** *sits at his computer, typing nervously.)*

FLYNN. 22 M4W Carrboro *(as he's typing)* You were the beautiful girl – *(to himself)* beautiful? That's the best I can do? No. Gorgeous? Jesus, I sound like a fucking fashionista. Stunning? Stunning works *(back to typing)* girl in the floral black dress at the Firefly on Saturday night. You danced with your friends and shot down a couple of guys that came over so, I thought you were a lesbian, but then you smiled at me a couple of times in a way that made me think you're not a lesbian.

(reading back over it) Yep. That'll woo her.

I was the guy in the flannel shirt watching you dance. In the span of fifteen minutes, you did the running man, waltzed with the older drunk man with a cane (who was still wearing his hospital bracelet) and did the most impressive high five with your friend I've ever seen. I went to the bathroom and then couldn't find you. I'd like to meet.

RAE. Reply to post. Hi. I stumbled on this. I think you might be talking about me. Or, I hope you are. And yes, I did notice you. And yes, I would like to meet.

SCENE 2

(A park bench. **FLYNN** *is sitting, nervously.* **RAE** *enters. She walks up to him from behind.)*

RAE. Hi.

(He stands and turns, his face dropping when he sees her.)

FLYNN. Hi. Can I help you?

RAE. Oh. I'm not sure. I'm supposed to be meeting someone-

FLYNN. 22 M for W?

RAE. Yes.

FLYNN. Am I who you expected to see?

RAE. Am I?

FLYNN. No.

RAE. Because you're not who I was expecting to...

FLYNN. Missed connection...

RAE. Yeah, apparently.

FLYNN. Shit.

RAE. Yeah...So, this is...

FLYNN. I'm Flynn.

RAE. Rae.

FLYNN. You were at the Firefly on Saturday?

RAE. Yes.

FLYNN. In a black dress?

RAE. A floral one.

FLYNN. And you made eye contact with a guy in a flannel shirt?

RAE. Yes. But, there was an obscene amount of flannel that night. Listen, maybe I should...

FLYNN. I'm surprised I didn't notice you.

RAE. From your post I gather you were distracted.

FLYNN. Look, I've never done this before; I was wasted when I wrote that.

RAE. Is that a lie?

FLYNN. Maybe.

RAE. Should I go? I should go.

FLYNN. I mean, you could stay, for a second. I mean you came all the way here from…your like home (oh God) – and…I came and-stay for a second.

RAE. I liked what you wrote. When I thought it was about me, I felt pretty special.

FLYNN. Why did you think it was you? I mean, did you do everything I wrote?

RAE. Most of it. I didn't waltz; I figured that was an oversight. I did dance near the old man with the cane, though. He smelled sour. And like yams.

FLYNN. And you did the running man?

RAE. Check.

FLYNN. And an epic high five?

RAE. My buddy, Lisa, got picked up by a guy who looked like a linebacker. I figured that warranted a celebratory hand gesture.

FLYNN. And then you just stumbled on my post?

RAE. I cruise craigslist with my roommates on Sunday mornings, it's tradition. Missed connections and bacon.

FLYNN. Breakfast of champions.

RAE. It's like tapping into the freak consciousness of the masses. Well, yours wasn't.

FLYNN. Thanks. This is just so bizarre.

RAE. I mean sure, but it's kinda nice to have a perfect stranger you thought you connected with think you are special, and that the subtleties of human interaction; glances and stuff, mean something. Something worth making a grand, digital gesture to find you.

FLYNN. I'm almost glad she didn't see it.

RAE. And I pegged you for a romantic.

FLYNN. Only when my life gets stale. And pretty girls –

RAE. Moisten?

FLYNN. I don't think "moisten" is the opposite of stale.

(awkward silence) (then:)

FLYNN. What was he like?

RAE. Who?

FLYNN. The guy who came here for.

RAE. I don't know, I didn't meet him. We just had some dark bar glances. No big.

FLYNN. Yeah.

RAE. So, who was she?

FLYNN. Just some girl.

RAE. Some, *stunning*, girl.

FLYNN. You ever see someone you don't know and they're so, alive or something, that you feel like you'd be better if you knew them? She looked like someone who…never mind.

RAE. What?

FLYNN. Collects vinyl and was taught to ballroom dance by her grandfather.

RAE. Excuse me?

FLYNN. You ever look at people and imagine the intricate details of their lives?

RAE. I'm not sure.

FLYNN. I do it with everyone I meet.

RAE. What do I look like?

FLYNN. You look like someone who sings beautifully in the shower.

RAE. Anywhere else?

FLYNN. Maybe. But, particularly in the shower.

RAE. Well, you look like someone who plays air guitar when no one's looking.

FLYNN. You look like someone who does yoga.

*(**RAE** makes a sound like a really loud, annoying buzzer on a game show when someone has just gotten a question wrong.)*

FLYNN. Does Zumba.

(**RAE** *makes an even longer buzzer sound.*)

Umm…rock climbed twice in the seventh grade.

RAE. You look like someone who talked to his stuffed animals as a kid.

FLYNN. New thing I talked to as a kid –

RAE. Imaginary friend, Juanita.

FLYNN. New name of imaginary friend –

RAE. Dionne Warwick.

FLYNN. You look like someone who…dries and saves flowers after you get them.

(*She makes the buzzer noise.*)

Smells flowers in full bloom.

(*She makes the buzzer noise.*)

Is allergic to flowers?

RAE. You look like someone who drove through both Carolinas without pants.

(**FLYNN** *makes buzzer noise.*)

Drove through both Carolinas wearing someone else's pants –

FLYNN. Ew. You look like someone who believes in Ouija boards.

RAE. You look like someone who would date a professional cat socializer.

(**FLYNN** *makes buzzer noise*)

Tried online dating.

FLYNN. Who hasn't? You look like someone who kisses girls when you're drunk.

RAE. New thing I do to girls when drunk.

FLYNN. Seriously?

RAE. You look like someone who wishes he were more turned on by that last statement.

(**FLYNN** *makes the buzzer noise.*)

FLYNN. You look like someone who would befriend the
neighborhood bird lady.

RAE. We all need friends. You look like someone who takes
his art seriously.

FLYNN. New thing I take seriously.

RAE. Everything.

FLYNN. Someone who cuts onions just to cry.

RAE. Someone who used to be in love.

FLYNN. Someone who wants to be.

(RAE makes the buzzer noise.)

Someone who lies.

RAE. You look like someone who dreams big but lives small.

FLYNN. Ouch.

RAE. I do, too.

*(They have a moment where they look at each other. He
reaches to touch her and kisses her. It's really awkward.
Like seventh-grade-behind-the-bleachers-tongue-caught-in-
a-tuba-player's-braces bad. They stop kissing.)*

RAE. Yeah.

FLYNN. I'm sorry. I just thought-

(He tries to kiss her again. She stops him.)

RAE. I'm going to –

FLYNN. Yeah. Nice to meet you.

RAE. Yep. Hey –

(RAE high fives him. It's epic.)

(end of play)

EDISON/TESLA: BRIAN/DAVE

Darren Miller and Kevin Mead

Edison/Tesla: Brian/Dave was produced as part of the 37th Annual Samuel French Off Off Broadway Short Play Festival at the Beckett Theater at Theater Row in New York City on October 27, 2012. The cast was as follows:

BRIAN .... Kevin Mead
DAVE .... Darren Miller
JENNIFER .... Emily Axford
SUSAN .... Laura Wilcox
MS. ANTONUCCI .... Shannon O'Neill
MIGUEL. .... Loni Yotan

CHARACTERS

JENNIFER – The hottest girl in the senior class. Besties with Suze. Every guy's got a crush on her...but ew they're gross. She's going to a state school in the Fall.

SUSAN – The smartest girl in the senior class. Besties with J. Has a crush on Dave...wait, what?! No she doesn't whatever shut up! She's going to Princeton in the Fall.

MS. ANTONUCCI – Has a husband and two dogs. Teaching was her second-choice career. She almost didn't come back to school after a car accident where she got side-swiped by a Coca Cola truck and almost died. She now realizes how precious life is, but lives in constant fear. She wears a neckbrace for the duration of the play.

MIGUEL – Captain of the hockey team. Loves his friends, loves rap music, hates homework. Screw homework, amiright? Let's party! Going to Dartmouth in the Fall (we know, we can't believe it either).

BRIAN – Former best friend of Dave. A recovering slacker, trying hard to finish out high school on a strong note. He'll probably run a business when he's older, or like...probably a bunch of em. Not as dumb as you think. Why would you think he's dumb at all, bro?! He's going to business school in the Fall.

DAVE – Former best friend of Brian. One of the smartest kids in class. But also one of the weirdest. He used to go to OzzFest every year, so what?? Whatever. His dream is to be a composer. He's going to Berkeley in the Fall.

PLAYWRIGHTS' NOTE

During their presentation, Brian and Dave alternate between speaking as themselves, and speaking as Edison and Tesla, respectively. The shifts between those characters are represented in the script by Brian and Dave putting on and taking off different hats – Brian with a nice Top Hat, and Dave with a weird hat, which could be any kind of unusual hat. Hats and distinctive physicality worked for us, but whatever works best for you would be just fine. Also, to our knowledge, all of the historical information referenced in this play is accurate. Lastly, this is a play about friendship. Sometimes friendships can be difficult and painful, but we think that mostly they're the best. Friendships don't always work out, but the good ones are always worth fighting for. If you're performing this play, we hope that you'll have fun with your friends while doing it.

ABOUT THE PLAYWRIGHTS

Darren Miller and Kevin Mead are co-founders of Melge, a film and entertainment production company, and are members of the comedy group "Mike Duffy." They write, act, direct, and produce for film and stage. They love beverages of all kinds.

(a high school classroom)

(AP American History. Spring. Senior year. **JENNIFER** *and* **SUSAN** *are finishing their presentation. The rest of the class,* **BRIAN**, **DAVE**, *and* **MIGUEL**, *wait in their seats.* **MS. ANTONUCCI** *sits, watching. She is wearing a neck brace. Upstage left is a chalkboard/whiteboard that says:)*

(AP American History end of year schedule:

~~*5/14 - review // 5/16 - test prep // 5/19 - AP Exam*~~

5/23 - Last Assignment - HIStory? YOURstory: Drop that textbook and tell us YOUR favorite untold story [1776-2000]!

5/26 - Graduation!)

SUSAN. Rosalind Franklin's contributions to the discovery of the DNA double helix model were completely overlooked by Watson and Crick. She was never given the credit she deserved, because she was a woman.

JENNIFER. Watson wrote years later that he was wrong in the way he treated Franklin.

SUSAN. But the damage was done and frankly Watson just exposed the sexist nature of the entire field of Science at the time. WHO KNOWS if it's even gotten better since then.

JENNIFER. In conclusion, we have benefited immensely from the work of Rosalind Franklin. But wouldn't the work of Rosalind Franklin and Watson & Crick have been much better and more influential if their rivalry had not ripped them apart?

SUSAN. Might they have been more successful if they hadn't violently swung their scientific swords at each other's throats, or clawed like rabid cats at each other's eyeballs?

JENNIFER. Yes.

JENNIFER & SUSAN. And that is our favorite untold story from American History. Thank you.

(obligatory applause from the class)

(MS. ANTONUCCI *stands.)*

MS. ANTONUCCI. Thank you Jennifer and Susan, that was a very insightful presentation.

JENNIFER & SUSAN. Thanks, Ms. Antonucci.

MS. ANTONUCCI. Does anyone in the class have any questions about their Untold Story?

(She looks out. No one raises their hand. She waits more.)

Despite what some of you seem to think, this still matters. Just because it's your last high school assignment doesn't mean it won't be graded.

MIGUEL. You're grading our questions?

MS. ANTONUCCI. Yes. As it clearly says on the assignment sheet, you'll be graded for your participation.

MIGUEL. Yo, the AP exam is over. This doesn't matter.

MS. ANTONUCCI. Yo...everything matters, Miguel. You might think it's just prom and graduation at this point, but tomorrow you might be driving down the highway to visit your fiance at work and get sideswiped by a Coca-Cola truck. Anything can happen.

MIGUEL. I don't care. I'm already going to Dartmouth.

MS. ANTONUCCI. You got into Dartmouth?

MIGUEL.. Yup. Thanks for the recommendation, Nooch.

MS. ANTONUCCI. Alright well next are Brian and Dave. And maybe after that I'll retire and visit Norway like I've always wanted to.

(BRIAN *and* **DAVE** *go to the front.)*

BRIAN. Thank you, Ms. Nooch. I just want to start by saying that, Jennifer, that was an excellent presentation. I feel like I've learned more in the last ten minutes than I have all year.

MS. ANTONUCCI. I hope you didn't write about Jennifer on your AP exam.

BRIAN. *(still to* **JENNIFER***)* I didn't, I wrote about the French and Indian War. By the way, are those new jeans?

DAVE. Hi, Jennifer. It's me, Dave. Great presentation you just gave. I didn't mean for that to rhyme.

SUSAN. I gave the presentation, too.

DAVE. Yeah good job Susan. Jennifer, you look really, really –

JENNIFER. You guys stop it!

MS. ANTONUCCI. Alright, guys. Please begin your presentation now.

BRIAN. Great. Our Untold Story is about the War of Currents. Hi. I am Brian Simmons. And this is Dave *Pantsin.*

DAVE. HANSON!

MIGUEL. PANTSIN! OH SNAP!

(Classmates laugh, stifle laughter.)

*(***SUSAN*** smiles.)*

JENNIFER. Ew. I don't even wanna think about that.

DAVE. The War of Currents occurred in the late eighteen hundreds with the rivalry between Thomas Edison and Nikola Tesla over competing types of electrical current distribution systems.

BRIAN. I will be presenting the work of one of the most influential inventors, innovators, and entrepreneurs of the modern era, Thomas Edison. To portray him, I will be wearing this hat.

(He holds up a really nice top hat.)

DAVE. I will be discussing the under-appreciated, under-valued, yet monumentally groundbreaking work of the first-ever mad scientist genius, Nikola Tesla. ...with this hat.

(pulls out really weird hat)

(BRIAN/DAVE *wear hats when speaking as Edison or Tesla.)*

BRIAN. That's a dumb hat.

DAVE. You're a dumb hat!

(JENNIFER *laughs.)*

MIGUEL. Aw SNAP! Hat burn!

DAVE. Why did you pair us together for this project? We've hated each other for almost all of high school.

MS. ANTONUCCI. Often a team can create something greater than what we are capable of alone. Sometimes our most trying experiences are the ones we learn from most.

(she touches her neck)

DAVE. Well we tried being friends for like ten years, and that turned out to be a huge waste of time for everyone.

BRIAN. I haven't even talked to this nerd in like three years. And then all of the sudden I have to spend four hours working in his basement. Do you have any idea what it smells like down there? He has a ferret.

DAVE. You shut up about Ferret Bueller!

(The class laughs.)

JENNIFER. Ew.

BRIAN. *(flirting)* I know. Gross right.

(JENNIFER *smiles back at him.)*

SUSAN. I think it's a clever name.

DAVE. *(to* **MS. ANTONUCCI***)* This is your fault!

MS. ANTONUCCI. No it's not. Just continue please.

DAVE. Fine.

BRIAN. Edison's Direct Current system was the standard in America during the early years of electricity. This is because Thomas Edison was the coolest and had the most friends.

DAVE. But then someone rose like a Phoenix from the shards of shattered incandescent light bulbs to show America the electric powered light.

(Acts out an explosion and assumes an impression of Nikola Tesla.)

It is I, Nikola Tesla!

(He assumes "common people".) (cheering) We love you! You're a genius! We don't know anything about you because we haven't given you a chance ever.

(as Tesla, with hat on) Well you will soon! For I am Nikola Tesla, inventor of the Alternating Current electricity distribution system! I am smart and not shy at all, and will respect you for who you are on the inside, Jennifer.

JENNIFER. What?

BRIAN. That never happened. Nobody loved you. *(as Edison, with hat on)* But everybody in the country loves me. I am Thomas Edison – inventor of a ton of amazing stuff! I gave Tesla his start at my company for $18 a week. He didn't know he could be making more because he's a dumb idiot from Yugoslavia. USA FOREVER.

*(**MIGUEL** cheers and tosses a bra and hits **BRIAN** in the face.)*

MS. ANTONUCCI. MIGUEL!

BRIAN. *(as Edison)* Thank you for your panties, commoner.

MIGUEL. You are welcome. Thomas Edison!

DAVE. *(as Tesla)* Oh hi, Thomas Edison. I know I'm just a "dumb idiot maintenance worker" but I couldn't help but notice how terrible your dynamos are. I can remake them into way more efficient machines that will save you tons of money. EASILY.

BRIAN. *(as Edison)* Yes! I love money! I will give you the privilege of rebuilding my Dynamos! Keep in mind that nobody would even know who you are if it wasn't for me.

DAVE. *(as Tesla)* Well I, Nikola Tesla, *actual* genius, will certainly do so!

(He mimes the process.)

(Thinking, notes being written in a notebook, wrenches moving, electricity buzzing through wires…)

(He makes an explosion sound).

DAVE. *(cont.)* There, I have done it! Your Dynamos are amazing now! You promised me fifty thousand dollars for my incredible work. I will take it and we will improve electricity throughout the world together because we have become best friends and surely you would never betray me.

BRIAN. *(as Edison)* Fifty thousand dollars? I never heard that! I, Thomas Edison, am a deaf person! That is a true thing about me! I will not pay you. And we were never friends, anyway. This is business. It's not my fault you got caught with your pants down. *(to **JENNIFER**)* And I can't help it if I am the best and most handsome businessman in the class, Jennifer.

SUSAN. You're not.

DAVE. *(as Tesla)* It is your fault I got caught with my pants down! You pulled them down! And you stole the girl I like. I mean, you stole all my inventions and stuff. Whatever. We could have ruled the world together, but instead, I quit.

MIGUEL. Oh no!

BRIAN. *(as Edison)* Fine! Go! I don't need you! I'm a successful innovator and you are a dork that no one knows.

MS. ANTONUCCI. Boys, I appreciate the creative approach to this historical tale, but I feel like we're veering off course a bit-

DAVE. Can you – um. Can you read this card real quick?

MS. ANTONUCCI. Is it relevant to this story?

DAVE. Yeah. Just…can you put this hat on?

*(**DAVE** pulls out a really big hat and hands it to her.)*

MS. ANTONUCCI. "Hello, America. It's me, your favorite friend and businessman, George Westinghouse. I am unable to perfect AC electricity due to the incompetence of my staff. Oh look, there is mad scientist genius Nikola Tesla, But what is he doing here? Should he not be in Menlo Park, New Jersey at the laboratories of Thomas Edison, my rival?"

DAVE. *(as Tesla)* No he should not! He should be spreading AC to the masses and taking down the Evil Thomas Edison, with you, George W.!

MS. ANTONUCCI. Okay. Here is so much money to continue your research as an employee of my company.

DAVE. *(as Tesla)* Thank you! Now I have the funds necessary to complete the most important innovation in history!

(Thinking, notes on a typewriter, wrenches, welding, super powerful electricity being transmitted over unprecedented distances!)

(He makes an explosion sound.)

I have done it! I have perfected the Alternating Current Electricity distribution system!

(as Commoners again) (cheering) We love you! Dave should get an A and Brian should fail your course! Alternating currents are our favorite! You are the one who deserves all of the panties!

*(**MIGUEL** throws panties up at **DAVE**.)*

Thank you for these panties and your continued support, Everyone in The Entire World.

BRIAN. Miguel! What the heck!

MIGUEL. I'm so confused! I think I really like this guy.

JENNIFER. Yeah it kind of seems like Tesla is the good guy here…I mean, he did all the work and is the smart one.

SUSAN. I think Tesla is cute and I really like his hat.

DAVE. Really? Thank you Jennifer!

BRIAN. *(as Edison)* Shut up everybody in the world, you are wrong! Tesla and Westinghouse are idiots.

MS. ANTONUCCI. Hey!

BRIAN. Alternating Current is dangerous for America. See here as I use alternating current to electrocute this elephant!

JENNIFER. What!?

BRIAN. Don't worry, Jennifer. I'll be okay, I know this Elephant is massive but I have everything under control.

SUSAN. That's not the point, that's animal cruelty.

BRIAN. It's 1890, Susan. And that elephant recently trampled four men! *(as Edison)* Also, if AC can kill this elephant and all these stray cats and dogs, imagine what it will do to us humans, you and I! These animals were Westinghoused, and you will be next!

(He acts out intense elephant electrocution as students flip out.)

SUSAN. Why are they still doing this presentation!? Is this even about history anymore?

MS. ANTONUCCI. Actually, this is accurate...

MIGUEL. They electrocuted stray cats and dogs!? Sweet!

BRIAN. Yes, Miguel. That was sweet. Thomas Edison's campaign to prove the danger of Alternating Current was successful. As T. to the E. once said, *(pulls out a note card)* "Hell, there are no rules here. We're trying to accomplish something." And I think that can mean a lot of things, Jennifer. I think there's some Direct Current electricity in those eyes.

JENNIFER. Can you never do that?

DAVE. Edison didn't accomplish anything! Edison was just a bully who had no problem ruining the reputation of his friends!

BRIAN. *(as Edison)* I am Thomas Edison! I've never ruined anything! I am the most prolific and well-known figure in Modern Science!

DAVE. *(as Tesla)* I am Nikola Tesla and you, Thomas Edison, totally F'd me!

BRIAN. *(as Edison)* You are a fool who is very dumb. I was making a hilarious joke when I agreed to pay you fifty thousand dollars. Also I am deaf. If I did say anything about money, I certainly did not *hear* it!

DAVE. Well it doesn't matter does it? Tesla was fine without Edison. Alternating Current powers almost every building in the world. So I guess *some* people can get totally screwed by their best friends and still be okay.

BRIAN. Yeah, then some people decide to get revenge and totally ruin their friend's academic career.

MS. ANTONUCCI. Guys, I don't think –

BRIAN. Look I don't know what you thought, but we were just friends cause we were neighbors.

DAVE. We were best friends! You knew I liked Jennifer and you screwed me over so you could get with her!

JENNIFER. Whoa, what?

MIGUEL. Hey, you guys talkin about the Hanson Pantsin'!?

DAVE. UGGHHH SHUT UP MIGUEL

MIGUEL. When you pantsed Dave on the freshman class camping retreat and everyone saw his penis?

JENNIFER. Ew oh my god gross.

SUSAN. Yeah…gross.

MIGUEL. You did kinda screw him. I mean, Dave…I've seen your balls, man. And like, so did everyone else.

MS. ANTONUCCI. That's enough Miguel.

MIGUEL. No, but seriously. Every single person in this room has seen Dave's junk. Except for you, Nooch. Oh, wait! Nooch was chaperone! Nooch, did you see Dave's junk too?

MS. ANTONUCCI. Miguel! What grade do you think you will get on your presentation about… *(she looks at her notebook)* "The Historical Importance of the Friendship between Wayne Gretzky and Mark Messier"?

MIGUEL. I don't know. A hundred.

MS. ANTONUCCI. No. Not one hundred. Also, where did your partner go? Travis has been gone since the end of your presentation.

MIGUEL. He went out. We were gonna get Subway foot-longs, but I hadda stay and throw panties.

MS. ANTONUCCI. You can all still fail this class. And your colleges will hear about that. Brian, Dave, please, wrap it up.

BRIAN. Well eventually they decided that Alternating Current would be better for buildings and houses and stuff. So I guess Tesla won the War of the Currents.

DAVE. But Tesla was forced to give up all the rights to Westinghouse anyway. He ended up alone and poor and died a mad man. So somehow the loser ends up with tons of inventions and money and the winner's life is ruined by a guy he thought was his best friend.

BRIAN. But after the War of the Currents, Edison realized that he had made a mistake by dismissing Tesla.

DAVE. That didn't happen. If that happened, why wouldn't Edison just apologize to Tesla for embarrassing him in front of the whole school, and then keep hanging out with him and stuff?

BRIAN. Because Edison was just doing what was right for business and for America. And he didn't realize he was ruining anything.

DAVE. Everyone saw my wiener!

MS. ANTONUCCI. Okay, you got everything out there, that's good. Everyone good? Everyone get everything off their chest? Alright then, you can go back to your seats and die happy now.

(They turn toward their seats, then.)

DAVE. No hang on we're not done!

(He puts on the Edison hat.)

MS. ANTONUCCI. OK. Great. Go for it.

DAVE. *(as Edison)* I'm Edison, and I was best friends with Tesla but then I totally screwed him, and Tesla died alone and I laughed about it with all my asshole friends.

BRIAN. *(as Tesla)* Hi, I'm Tesla. Instead of forgiving Edison for that one mistake I will take revenge by totally sabotaging his entire high school career.

MS. ANTONUCCI. OK, you're just talking about yourselves. At least lose the hats and be yourselves.

DAVE. *(as BRIAN)* Oh hi I'm Brian and my best friend and I like the same girl. Good thing he's a nerd and I am the cool dude. I wear a letterman jacket now.

BRIAN. *(as DAVE)* Oh hi, I'm Dave. I just sit in the back of classrooms and draw creepy shit on my desk and go to OzzFest. How come no one likes me??

DAVE. No one likes me cause they have to think about me naked every time they see me in the hallway. And I'm not "drawing creepy shit" I'm composing music. Does everyone think I'm drawing creepy shit!?

(Classmates murmur "Yes".)

MS. ANTONUCCI. Well, okay, that settles that!

BRIAN. *(as DAVE)* Hello. It is me Dave again. I have changed since last year. I still want to be friends with Brian. Hey, Brian, I see that you are having difficulty in European history. Do you need help writing the term paper on the Reformation? *(as BRIAN)* Are you sure Dave? I mean, is that allowed? *(as DAVE)* Totally, it is allowed, Brian! You focus on baseballs and being in the play. I'll just write your paper for you. *(as BRIAN)* Oh, awesome, Dave, you're awesome. *(as DAVE)* JUST KIDDING. The paper is totally bogus. After the well written thesis paragraph, it's just six pages of Shaquille O'Neill's tweets. Then you'll go on academic probation and spend the rest of high school getting straight A's to make up for it.

JENNIFER. Ms. Antonucci, can the rest of us go? This isn't really a presentation anymore. I'm really uncomfortable.

BRIAN. This isn't about you Jennifer!

DAVE. Yes it is! It's all about her!

SUSAN. Ms. Antonucci, please! Can we please go?

MS. ANTONUCCI. Brian. Dave. Sit down. Your presentation's been over for a while now. Your Untold Story has been told. Vividly. Now, before everyone leave, I would just like to say –

DAVE. Wait, no! Jennifer you have to hear this.

MS. ANTONUCCI. David, please do not continue speaking. You get a B. High School is over.

DAVE. Hi Jennifer. It's me, Dave. Umm…I know I'm a weirdo and no one likes me. But I've always liked you. Like, like-liked you. Your hair is good and you care a lot about cool things and you're very beautiful and WILLYOUGOTOSENIORFORMALWITHME?

JENNIFER. What?–

BRIAN. Don't answer him! Hear me out first. I only pantsed Dave to impress you, and then we hooked up and I didn't call you, but it was just because I wanted you to think that I was the coolest. But I'm not the coolest. I know I messed up. But high school is over and this is my last chance. Come to Senior Formal with me.

JENNIFER. I'm not going to senior prom with either of you. I'm going with Susan.

MIGUEL. Oh SHIT! Lesbians!

SUSAN. Shut up Miguel! No one even likes you, they just use you for parties cause your parents are rich, and they don't love you so they're never home.

JENNIFER. We're not lesbians. We're going to the formal together because we're best friends. And every single guy at this school is a huge asshole. How do you think this works? You hook up with a girl once at a party, then you treat her like crap, and then you're in love? Or you watch her weirdly from a distance without saying anything to her for years, and then she notices you like her and she likes you back? You guys are totally conceited, you think everything is about you and that everyone cares so much about your stupid friendship.

You're not gonna be friends anymore? Great, we all get it, and we don't give a shit.

MS. ANTONUCCI. And...good. You've got your answers. You probably could have gotten those answers three years ago. You're lucky you got another chance. Don't waste your lives.

DAVE. Hey, Susan. Hi. It's me, Dave. Would you maybe want to go to formal with me?

SUSAN. No! Seriously? I'm going with Jennifer. You know, my best friend who you both just asked to formal right in front of me? Dave, I liked you for three years. I always knew you were composing music. I thought you were drawing weird shit too, but I liked it. But you just ignored me like everyone else. I would have gone to prom with you up until literally thirty seconds ago. Idiot.

MIGUEL. Oh SNAP, terrible timing, Dave.

SUSAN. And hey all you jerks, you know who didn't ignore me? Princeton. If you need to find me, that's where I'll be.

(*JENNIFER and* **SUSAN** *do a very specific high-five, and start to leave.*)

MS. ANTONUCCI. Everyone stop high-fiving and putting on hats and talking about Dave's...features. I know this is the last day of classes, and everyone's all lubed up for prom and trying to "settle scores"...and that's good. That's what you should do. Because you don't know what could happen on your way home from school. You could get sideswiped by a massive truck full of cola and die. But obviously Brian and Dave that was extremely inappropriate and you made everyone very uncomfortable. Meet me in the Principal's office in five minutes. I hope you all make it through the summer and drive to college as safely as possible.

MIGUEL. You know, Nooch, I don't know if I see it that way. All this fighting, and who likes who, and who screwed who, and everyone seeing Dave's meat. None of this stuff really matters. I mean, Dave it's okay that I've seen your dong. It's who you are, bro. But I'll probably never see you again. After graduation, we'll all live in different cities with new friends, and we'll probably just drift apart. We'll find new things, and then those things will end, and we'll move onto new things after that. And then maybe we do get side-swiped by a Coca-Cola truck and die. But until then, each thing shapes us, preparing us for the new thing ahead.

MS. ANTONUCCI. Wow, Miguel...you're right. I can't keep living in fear of the Coca-Cola truck. I need to drive my own truck. That's the most insightful thing you've ever –

TRAVIS. *(offstage)* Yo, Miguel, heads up.

(A subway sandwich is tossed on stage. He catches it.)

MIGUEL. Ahhh SNAP. SUBWAY FOOTLONG!

(He sprints offstage.)

MIGUEL *(offstage)* Travis, wait up, are there sweet peppers on this?

*(***MS. ANTONUCCI*** *sighs.)*

MS. ANTONUCCI. Okay.

(She leaves. **JENNIFER** *and* **SUSAN** *follow.* **BRIAN** *and* **DAVE** *stand there.)*

BRIAN. I kind of stopped liking Jennifer like last year anyway.

DAVE. Yeah. Me too.

BRIAN. I um...heard you got into Berkely.

DAVE. Oh. Yeah...heard you're going to business school

BRIAN. Yea...I guess that presentation didn't go so well.

(They look through their note cards.)

DAVE. Actually I think I covered everything I was gonna say...

BRIAN. I have a conclusion written out... *(reading from note-card)* The War of the Currents drove these two great men apart. Their rivalry led them to create amazing things on their own, but it ruined the potential for them to create something amazing together. Who knows what history books would say if instead of being famous rivals, they stayed the most incredible innovating partners of all time? Would they then have achieved even greater greatness?

(**DAVE** *considers.*)

DAVE. It doesn't matter.

BRIAN & DAVE. Thank you.

(blackout)

(end of play)